For James

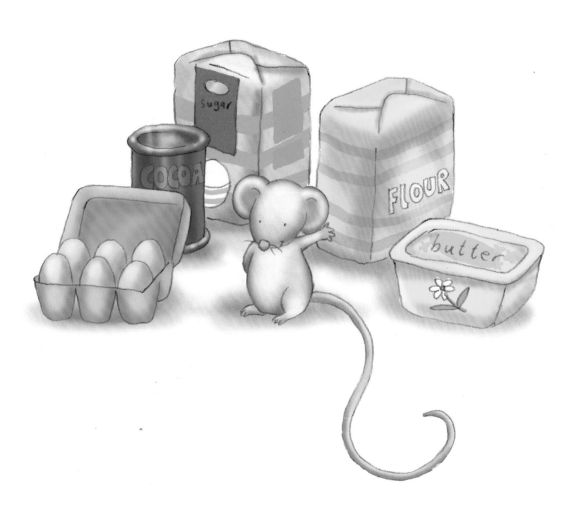

Published in 2010 by Windmill Books, LLC
303 Park Avenue South, Suite # 1280, New York, NY 10010-3657

Adaptations to North American Edition © 2010 Windmill Books
Copyright © Tiberius Publishing 2007
The word Tiberius is a trademark of Keith Harvey.

First Published in 2007 by Tiberius Publishing

CREDITS:
Text: Keith Harvey
Illustrator: Heather Kirk

Library of Congress Cataloging-in-Publication Data

Harvey, Keith.
 Tiberius and the chocolate cake / written by Keith Harvey ; illustrated by Heather Kirk.
    p. cm. – (Tiberius tales)
 Summary: Tiberius the mouse decides to bake a cake on a rainy day, but when his friends join in to help, the cake turns out much smaller than expected.
 ISBN 978-1-60754-832-4 (library binding) – ISBN 978-1-60754-836-2 (pbk.) – ISBN 978-1-60754-840-9 (6-pack)
 [1. Mice–Fiction. 2. Animals–Fiction. 3. Baking–Fiction.] I. Kirk, Heather, ill. II. Title.
 PZ7.H26757Tg 2010
 [E]–dc22
                                        2009041106

Manufactured in the United States of America

CPSIA Compliance Information: Batch #BW10W: For futher information contact Windmill Books, New York, New York at 1-866-478-0556.

Tiberius
and the
Chocolate Cake

Written by Keith Harvey

Illustrated by Heather Kirk

alphabet
soup™

an imprint of
WINDMILL BOOKS™
New York

Tiberius woke up and looked out the window.
He rubbed his eyes and looked again.
"Oh no, it's raining," he said.
"What am I going to do today?"
"I'll make a chocolate cake and invite all my friends
to a tea party."

Tiberius opened the front door, put up
his umbrella and went jumping and
splashing in and out of the puddles
on his way down the lane.
He came to the signpost.
One way pointed right
and the other way pointed left.

Left

Right

"Which way should I go
today? I'd better go left
and down to the village to
get the ingredients for my
chocolate cake."

When he got to the store there was Mrs. Johnson, the storekeeper, behind the counter.
"Hello Tiberius," she said. "What can I do for you today?"

"Well," said Tiberius slowly. "I'm going to make a big chocolate cake for all my friends and I need the ingredients."

"Okay," said Mrs. Johnson. "You'll need some flour, sugar, eggs, butter and some chocolate powder."
She put the ingredients into a big bag and gave them to Tiberius.

As he started to leave the store he turned and said, "Just one other thing, Mrs. Johnson. How do I make it?"

"It's very easy," said Mrs. Johnson. "First you mix the butter and sugar together. Then you stir in the eggs and then the flour and chocolate powder. But remember to stir the mixture well." Tiberius thanked Mrs. Johnson, picked up his shopping bag, put up his umbrella and hurried back home.

When he arrived home, who was sitting outside his house but Sneaky Cat, Croaky Crow and his special friend Drag.

"What are you all doing here?" he said.
"It was raining," said Drag, "and we didn't know what to do, so we thought you would have some good ideas."
"I do," said Tiberius. "I'm going to make a chocolate cake and you can help me."

"What a good idea," said Croaky Crow as they all trooped inside. "What do we do first?" asked Sneaky Cat. "Everyone must wash their hands," said Tiberius, "then follow me into the kitchen."

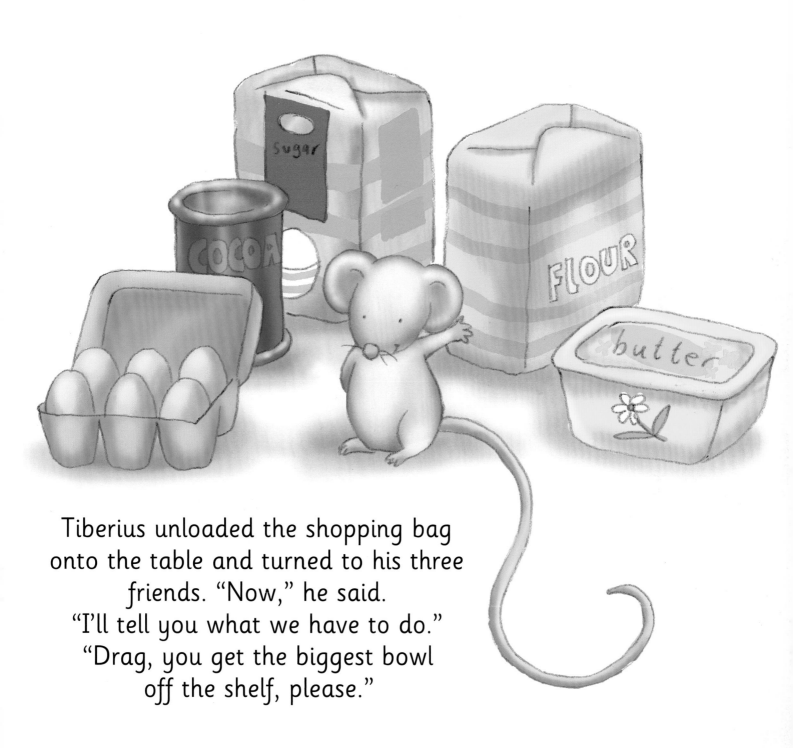

Tiberius unloaded the shopping bag
onto the table and turned to his three
friends. "Now," he said.
"I'll tell you what we have to do."
"Drag, you get the biggest bowl
off the shelf, please."

"Croaky Crow, you get the measuring cups from the cupboard, please. Sneaky Cat, please get the cake pan - it's in the cupboard underneath the sink."

When they had collected their equipment they gathered around the kitchen table. "Now," said Tiberius. "We must first mix the butter and sugar together."

"I can do that with my tail," said Sneaky Cat.
"It would be better if I stirred it with my tail," said Drag.
"It's bigger."

"Stop being silly," said Croaky Crow. "You can't stir it with your tails. We must have some spoons."
"You're right," said Tiberius. "Drag, please get three spoons out of the drawer and give one to each of us."

When all the ingredients were in the bowl everyone began to stir. "Stir it well," said Tiberius. "I am going to grease the big pan to put the cake batter into." They stirred and stirred and stirred.

14

"This looks good," said Drag. He stirred too hard and a bit of the cake batter shot out onto his hand. "Oh dear," he said as he licked it off. "That was a little messy." But then a smile came over Drag's face.

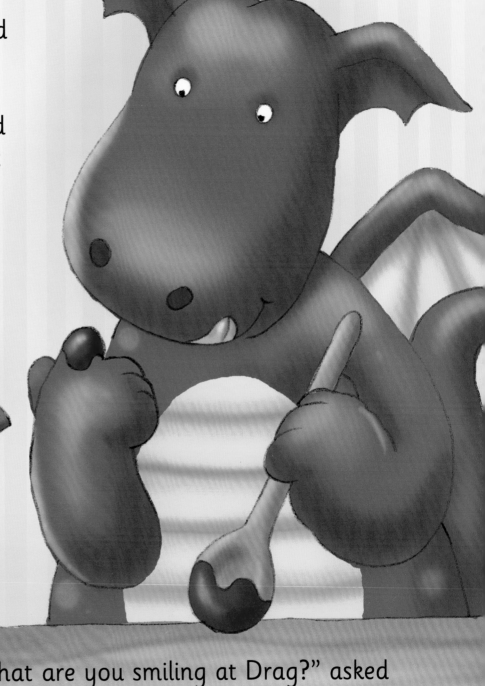

"What are you smiling at Drag?" asked Croaky Crow. "That tasted really, really delicious," he replied.

15

Then he licked his spoon that was covered with the chocolate batter and smiled again.
"I'm going to try that," said Sneaky Cat and he licked his spoon.

"Well, if you're going to have a taste of the batter before it's baked then so am I," said Croaky Crow, and he had the biggest spoonful of them all.

"Yummy, this is fun on a rainy day." They all went on having a stir and a lick, a stir and a lick, a stir and a lick.

17

"The baking pan is ready," said Tiberius as he walked back into the room. "Pass me the bowl of chocolate cake batter, please."

Sneaky Cat, Croaky Crow and Drag all looked at each other rather sheepishly, then pushed the bowl toward Tiberius.

Tiberius looked into the bowl. "What happened?" he said. "What's happened to my cake?" "Err, um we stirred a little too hard," said Drag. "How strange," said Tiberius. "I thought there would be far more batter than this, my cake pan is far too big. I'll have to use a smaller one."

The three friends looked at each other. Drag looked out the
window. The sun was now shining.
"I think we should all go for a walk before Tiberius realizes what
has happened." he said. Tiberius returned with another baking
pan. "We are all thinking of going for a walk," said Drag.
"What a good idea!" said Tiberius.

"I'll put this in the oven and we can
eat it when we get back."
So off the four friends went
for a long walk.

After a while Tiberius thought it was time for them to go back and share the cake. "I don't think I'll come," said Drag. "I don't know why, but I just don't feel very hungry." "How strange, neither do I," said Sneaky Cat. "I don't either," said Croaky Crow. "But I think I know why," and he winked at the other two. "I think we had better just see you tomorrow, Tiberius," they all said in unison. "Enjoy your cake."

When Tiberius got home and took the cake out of the oven he just couldn't understand why it was so small.

But we know why, don't we?